DISNEP
FAIRIES

Beck
Beyond
the
Sea

Beck Beyond the Sea

WRITTEN BY
KIMBERLY MORRIS

ILLUSTRATED BY
DENISE SHIMABUKURO
& THE DISNEY STORYBOOK ARTISTS

A STEPPING STONE BOOK™
RANDOM HOUSE 🏠 NEW YORK

Published in the United States by Random House Children's
Books, a division of Random House, Inc., New York, and in
Canada by Random House of Canada Limited, Toronto, in
conjunction with Disney Enterprises, Inc. RANDOM HOUSE and
colophon are registered trademarks and A STEPPING STONE
BOOK and colophon are trademarks of Random House, Inc.

Library of Congress Cataloging-in-Publication Data

Morris, Kimberly.
Beck beyond the sea / written by Kimberly Morris ; illustrated by
Denise Shimabukuro and the Disney Storybook Artists.
p. cm.
"A Stepping Stone book."
SUMMARY: After watching the Explorer Birds pass her by, Beck uses
some of Vidia's enhanced fairy dust to help her fly faster so she can
travel with the birds beyond the boundaries of Never Land.

ISBN: 978-0-7364-2456-1 (pbk.)

[1. Fairies—Fiction. 2. Flight—Fiction. 3. Adventure and adventurers—
Fiction.] I. Shimabukuro, Denise, ill. II. Disney Storybook Artists.
III. Title.
PZ7.M7881635Be 2007   [Fic]—dc22
2006039273

www.randomhouse.com/kids/disney
Printed in the United States of America
10 9 8 7 6 5

All About Fairies

IF YOU HEAD toward the second star on your right and fly straight on till morning, you'll come to Never Land, a magical island where mermaids play and children never grow up.

When you arrive, you might hear something like the tinkling of little bells. Follow that sound and you'll find Pixie Hollow, the secret heart of Never Land.

A great old maple tree grows in Pixie Hollow, and in it live hundreds of fairies and sparrow men. Some of them can do water magic, others can fly like the wind, and still others can speak to animals. You see, Pixie Hollow is the Never fairies' kingdom, and each fairy who lives there has a special, extraordinary talent.

Not far from the Home Tree, nestled in the branches of a hawthorn, is Mother Dove, the most magical creature of all. She sits on her egg, watching over the fairies, who in turn watch over her. For as long as Mother Dove's egg stays well and whole, no one in Never Land will ever grow old.

Once, Mother Dove's egg *was* broken. But we are not telling the story of the egg here. Now it is time for Beck's tale. . . .

Beck
Beyond
the
Sea

IT WAS A BEAUTIFUL AFTERNOON, cool and clear with a golden glow. Every once in a while, the breeze would puff. It sent dandelion fluff through the air and lifted the tendrils of Beck's hair to tickle her ear.

Beck sighed happily and listened in on a conversation between a pair of chameleons. Beck was an animal-talent fairy, and she could communicate with all the creatures in Never Land. She understood the meaning of every buzz, hiss, peep, coo, growl, purr, bark, and honk.

The chameleons were trying to decide whether they looked better in yellow or orange. Beck was about to offer her opinion—which was that you could never go wrong with basic green—

when she spotted a forest boar. She had never seen that boar before. He looked very intent as he trotted along the main path.

Beck flew quietly over him and watched him from above. Where was he going? What was he doing? Was he friend or foe? She followed the boar until he turned off the path and dove under some brush.

Beck flew lower. Where had he gone?

She saw a bush shake. Then a mound of dirt rumbled. Was that him? Yes! Wait! *There* he was. No! There? No!

The boar was gone. He had probably ducked into one of the tunnels below Pixie Hollow. Many years before, the animal-talent fairies had built a maze of underground tunnels that only they could find their way around. Beck hoped the boar wouldn't get lost.

"*Snort!*"

The boar popped up from the underbrush. Beck suddenly found herself face to eyeball with him. She was so startled, she somersaulted backward and landed in a sprawl on a broad blade of elephant grass.

The boar made a series of boar sounds. "*Snort! Grunt! Snort! Snort! Grunt! Snuffle! Snort!*"

Now, a pots-and-pans-talent fairy, such as Tink, or a water-talent fairy, such as Rani, would have heard a lot of scary boar noises. But remember, Beck was an animal-talent fairy. Even though she had never met this boar before, she knew what the noise was—good-natured laughter. The boar was not an enemy.

Beck sat up, straightened her tunic, and flew closer. The boar snuffled a bit, but Beck understood him perfectly. "Aha! Caught you," he said. "You're following me, aren't you?"

"Yes," Beck answered. "Are you angry? I know spying is bad manners."

"I'm not angry. But why are you following me? Have I done something wrong?"

"No, no, no!" Beck answered. "I was just curious. Whenever I see strangers, I wonder where they came from and where they are going."

The boar lifted his hairy upper lip to

show a set of long, sharp white teeth.

Another fairy might have mistaken this for a menacing snarl. But Beck saw a friendly smile. The boar told her, "I'm from the eastern tip of Never Land, and I'm on my way to the western side of the Never Land forest. There are truffles there that taste like clouds dipped in joy. And when the rain falls, it makes a noise like nothing you've ever heard. It's just like music. You can settle under a rotten log and listen all afternoon. Here's the song I heard on my last visit."

He threw back his head and began to sing in his snuffly boarlike way. *"Snuffle snuffle snort snort grunt grunt snoooooorrrrt!"*

Beck felt chills up and down her

spine. Even through his snorts and snuf-
fles, she could hear the music plainly. It
was a strange, beautiful melody.

When he was done, she clapped.
"The rain never makes music like that in
Pixie Hollow," she said. "I wonder why."

"Different plants. Different dirt.
Different sound," the boar explained.
"It's a beautiful place, Pixie Hollow, but
you just don't get the music here that
you get in the western forest. Or the
truffles, either."

Beck sighed. "I wish I could hear a
rain song."

"Come with me," he invited. "It takes
only a few weeks to get there."

Beck shook her head sadly. "In Pixie
Hollow, there's just enough of every-

thing. No more, no less. Every fairy gets one teacup of fairy dust a day. My dust wouldn't take me that far. Without it, I can't fly."

"Well, you can walk. And when you get tired, you can ride on my back."

Beck was touched. That was a very nice offer. "I wish I could. But I can't. If I left, who would take care of Mother Dove?"

"I've heard of her. Wonderful bird. Love to meet her sometime. Not today, though. I've got to get going before the truffle season is over." He twitched an ear. "Good-bye."

"Good-bye," Beck said as the boar turned and trotted off.

She was still watching him when she

heard a heavy rustle above her. She looked up. A flock of strange blue-and-yellow-striped birds passed overhead.

Those birds fascinated Beck. They always flew fast and stayed in a perfect star formation that turned in the sky like a pinwheel.

But they never stopped to visit. They moved right past Pixie Hollow. What kind of birds were they? Where were they going? As she watched, they passed over the treetops and soared into the distant sky.

Beck flew to Mother Dove's nest in the hawthorn tree at the edge of Pixie Hollow. As always, Mother Dove looked contented sitting in her nest on her magic blue egg.

"Hello, Mother Dove!" Beck said. "Is there anything you need?"

Mother Dove cooed happily. "Just a glimpse of you. And now I have it."

Beck felt her mouth curve into a smile. Knowing that Mother Dove loved her and needed her made Beck feel special. Without Mother Dove, there would be no Never Land. She was the source of all its magic.

Beck looked up again, watching the birds in the sky. "How big is the world, Mother Dove?"

Mother Dove ruffled her feathers a bit and settled herself more comfortably. "Bigger than we can imagine."

Beck closed her eyes and tried to imagine. Mother Dove was right. She couldn't. "Imagining is hard work," Beck said with a laugh. "It's making me hungry."

"Why don't you go get a cup of tea

and a muffin?" Mother Dove suggested.

"All right, then," Beck agreed. "I'll be back later."

"Don't hurry," Mother Dove said kindly. "I'm fine here. I'm always fine."

Beck took to the air again. She passed over Queen Clarion's gazebo, the dairy barn, the fairy-dust mill, and Havendish Stream.

She flew into the lobby of the Home Tree and fluttered into the tearoom.

Every day, baking-talent fairies baked perfect pastries. Decoration-talent fairies covered the tables with fresh flower petals. And laundry-talent fairies folded the leaf napkins in new and amazing ways.

That day, the napkins were folded

into star shapes. They kind of reminded Beck of the blue-and-yellow birds in their star formation.

The tearoom was almost empty. A few mining-talent fairies huddled together over a map. Beck was too shy to join them. She didn't really know anything about mining. Besides, they looked busy and serious about their work.

So Beck helped herself to some butter cookies from the buffet and darted out the window. She flew straight to her favorite perch. She called it the Tip-Top. It was the highest branch on the tallest tree in Pixie Hollow. Beck landed lightly.

"Hello," said a friendly voice behind her. "What are you doing way up here?"

Beck turned. Terence, a dust-talent sparrow man, was sitting only a twig or two away.

"What are *you* doing up here?" she countered. "I thought this was *my* special place."

Terence laughed. "I come up here for the view."

Beck handed him a butter cookie and grinned. "Me too. Do you ever wonder what's over there . . . and over there . . . and over there?" She waved her hands comically in a circle.

Terence looked out at the forest and mountains beyond Pixie Hollow.

"Sometimes," he said. "But mostly I just like to be here." He turned back to Beck. "Have you ever heard of a sparrow man called Spinner?"

Beck shook her head.

"He was curious like you. He said

there was a big world outside Pixie Hollow and he had to see it."

"And did he?"

Terence nodded. "He did. He was gone for the longest time, because of course, he ran out of dust and had to walk. He was gone so long we thought he'd been eaten by a hawk, or died of disbelief. But then one day he walked back into Pixie Hollow. He looked as shabby as an old tunic but merry as a bell. He said he had seen the most marvelous things. A sea with waves striped with different colors. And a desert with sand that talked."

Beck felt her heart begin to beat faster. How wonderful it would be to travel and see all those things!

"Of course, we didn't believe a word of it," Terence added.

Beck's face fell. "Why not?"

Terence laughed. "Because he was a tall-tale-telling-talent sparrow man. He actually claimed he'd found a truffle that tasted like a cloud dipped in joy and heard a rainstorm that sounded like music. He said he'd met butterflies the size of Clumsies. Oh, and this is a good one. He said he'd seen trees that grew upside down and flopped on the ground at night to sleep. He said in the morning, they straightened up and stretched their roots in the air just like somebody yawning."

Beck remembered what the boar had said about truffles and rain. "Maybe they *weren't* just stories. Maybe they were true," she argued. "Where is Spinner now? I wish I could talk to him."

Terence shrugged. "He disappeared soon after he came back. We figured he'd gone traveling again."

They heard a rustle overhead. It was another flock of blue-and-yellow birds in pinwheel formation.

Beck jumped up. This time they weren't flying over! They were coming in for a landing. The formation broke into a hundred separate fluttering birds. They landed in the treetops, laughing and joking.

Beck cleared her throat. As an animal-talent fairy, she felt it was her duty to greet them. "Hello," she said. "Welcome."

The leader of the flock puffed out her chest and flapped her wings. She opened her beak and squawked a series of birdcalls.

Now, Terence, as a dust-talent sparrow man, heard something that sounded like this: "*Caw caw whoooop! Twoooieeee! sreek!*"

But Beck understood the flock leader perfectly. What *she* heard was this: "Hello! We were told that this is Pixie Hollow and that we would be welcome. We'd like to eat some of your berries and drink from your streams—if you don't mind."

"We don't mind at all," Beck answered. She was delighted to have a chance to meet these strange birds.

"Where are you from? Where is your home?"

The birds laughed.

Beck smiled. "Did I say something funny?"

The flock leader's eye twinkled. "We are Explorer Birds. Our home is wherever we happen to land. And wherever we land, we feel at home." She sipped some dew from a cupped leaf. "My name is Goway," she said after swallowing.

"I'm Beck."

Goway cocked her head, looking at Beck's wings. "Are you a bird?"

"No. I'm a fairy!"

"Then how is it that you speak Bird?"

"I'm an animal-talent fairy," Beck

explained. She leaned forward eagerly. "But tell me something. Have you ever seen a sea with striped waves? Or heard sand talk? Or eaten a truffle that—"

The thundering sound of a hundred pairs of wings drowned out Beck's soft voice. The birds were in flight again, circling and chasing each other.

Goway gave Beck a little bow. "Sorry. Wish I had time to talk. But this flock is restless. I'd better go up front and get them moving." She beat her wings against the air. Seconds later, the birds had fallen into formation and were spinning away.

Beck opened her lips to say goodbye but bit back the word. Why not go with them? Instead of trying to *imagine* the size of the world, why not see it for herself? Or at least as much as she could see in a day.

She shouted, "Wait! Wait! I want to go with you." She leaped into the air and flew as fast as she could.

"Where are you going?" she heard Terence call. "Hey, what did they say?"

Beck didn't pause to answer. She couldn't. No time. The birds were already high in the air and yards away. She lowered her head into the wind and beat her wings as hard as she could. Faster . . . faster . . . faster . . .

But no matter how fast she flew, she couldn't catch up. They were too quick. Finally, she gave up. She landed on a branch and watched them disappear into the distance.

Her wings had come to a stop. But her mind was racing and spinning . . . just like a pinwheel.

3

"Wing extenders!" Tink exclaimed.

The inside walls of Tink's metal teapot workshop arched up and curved over like a high vaulted ceiling. Tink's surprised cry bounced off them and echoed through the workshop.

Beck nodded. "I think my wings are too short. If I had longer wings, I could fly faster."

"Beck, you're not a fast-flying-talent fairy," Tink argued. "Why do you need to fly any faster?"

"I want to keep up with the birds," Beck explained.

"That makes sense," Tink agreed. "You *are* an animal-talent fairy. So I suppose keeping up with birds *would* be a good thing." Tink pulled her bangs, the way she always did when she had a problem to solve.

"I know!" She snapped her fingers and hurried to a big pile of scrap metal.

Clang! Clank! Clink! Boooinnng! went the scrap metal as Tink sorted through it. "Twire brought these over to see if I could use them for anything," she shouted over the noise.

She pulled a pair of long wire frames from the pile. "Let's see what I can do." Tink grabbed her tinker's hammer and began to pound.

Clang! Bang! Clang! Bang!

Beck covered her ears.

"There!" Tink gave the frames one last little knock with her hammer.

Pong!

"Try this!" She lifted the lightweight wire frames off the worktable and placed them across Beck's shoulders. The wire frames fit over Beck's wings and made them twice as long.

"That ought to do it." Tink nodded, and her bangs bounced. "Now all we need are a few yards of gauze and a couple of sewing-talent fairies, and you're good to go."

An hour later, Beck was back at the Tip-Top, wearing her wing extenders. The sewing-talent fairies had done a beautiful job of stretching gauze over Tink's wire

frames. Beck's test flight had brought her to the Tip-Top in record time.

It almost made her wish she were a fast-flying-talent fairy instead of an animal-talent fairy. It was exciting to move through the air twice as fast as usual.

She heard a sound in the distant wind. She looked up. *Yes!* It was another flock of Explorer Birds. Beck stood, ready for flight.

As soon as they came into view, she shot into the air. Never had she flown so fast. Within seconds, she was catching up with the birds. "Hello!" she cried. "Mind if I join you?" She moved to the right and tried to join the flock. But the wing extenders made Beck clumsy.

Whap! Whap!

Uh-oh! Her wing extenders knocked, jostled, and swatted the birds around her. They didn't like it one bit.

"OUCH!"

"WHAT IS THAT? SOME KIND OF HAWK?"

"HEY, STOP IT! WHO ARE YOU SHOVING?"

"YOU'RE NOT A BIRD! WHAT DO YOU THINK YOU'RE . . ."

Suddenly, Beck found herself twirling through the air in a tangle of wings, gauze, feathers, and beaks. She felt a series of angry pecks on her head and arms. The Explorer Birds were trying to drive her away.

Beck gave her wings one huge hard flap and shot out of the tangle.

As soon as she was out of it, the Explorer Birds got into line again. They turned and flew away from her as fast as they could.

Beck wobbled back to the Tip-Top. Her wing extenders were bent and torn. She shrugged them off. But she wasn't giving up. She had another idea for flying with the birds. It was a much better one, too.

"*Now you want a sleigh?*" Tink looked at Beck as though she were crazy.

"Please help me, Tink! I know *this* will work. Look." Beck leaned over Tink's worktable and sketched on a torn leaf. "Like this. See? But not made out of

Never pewter. Made out of grass and bark. So it will be lightweight."

Tink pulled her bangs. "If it's not made out of metal, I won't be of much help. Let's go see the grass-weaving-talent fairies." She folded up the sketch and put it in her pocket. Then they set off to find others to help them.

In the end, it took several fairy talent groups to make the sleigh. The measuring-talent fairies measured Beck from head to toe and all around. The grass-weaving-talent fairies wove grass, reeds, and dandelion fluff into a seat and a harness. The carpenter-talent fairies built a frame out of the thinnest bark. And the art-talent fairies painted everything blue to match the sky. When they were all done, Beck sat in a beautiful sleigh just big enough for one fairy.

It was graceful, delicate, and light as a feather. Beck knew that any bird would be proud to pull it.

Fawn looked at it and sighed. "Shall we call one of the ravens and ask him to take you for a test ride?"

"No! No! L-l-let me! Me. Oh, p-p-pleeeaaase!"

They all looked up and saw Twitter fluttering toward them. The little hummingbird flew all around the sleigh. "Let me pull it . . . please. I can do it. I promise. Let me. Let me."

"But, Twitter," Beck said, "you've never pulled a sleigh before. It might be hard."

"Please let me have a turn. Please? I'm very strong for a hummingbird."

Beck whispered to Fawn, "I don't want to hurt his feelings. It'll probably be too heavy for him."

"Just let him try," Fawn whispered back. "He'll give up soon and then we can call the ravens."

Beck turned to Twitter and spoke in Bird. "Okay. Great! I can't think of anyone I'd rather fly with."

Twitter happily thrust his wings into the grass harness. "Here we go!"

Beck had hardly had time to settle herself when the little hummingbird darted into the air and the sleigh jerked. Beck's heart thumped, and she almost dropped the reins.

At first the sleigh didn't move. But Twitter flapped his wings faster and faster. Little by little, the sleigh rose into the air.

The fairies cheered as it climbed higher.

Once it was up, the breeze helped things along. Pretty soon, Twitter was pulling the sleigh through the air, darting this way and that.

"This is fun!" Twitter shouted.

It *was* fun. But it was also a pretty bouncy ride. Beck realized that Twitter's hummingbird style of flying wasn't the best for pulling a sleigh. Twitter darted left . . . then right . . . then left again. They flew through a gust of wind. Uh-oh! The sleigh began to tip. A second gust of wind caused it to teeter back and forth. Beck was thrown against the side. The sudden shift of her weight upset the balance. She felt her stomach flip as the sleigh turned upside down in the air and she fell out.

Oh, no!

Beck hurtled headfirst toward the ground. Faster and faster she fell. She struggled to open her wings and fly, but it was hard to do while falling upside down. Beck looked below her. The ground and trees came rushing up to meet her. She took one last look at the world speeding past and then squeezed her eyes shut.

4

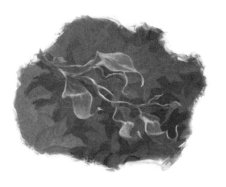

CRASH! BOOM! Riiip! Sproiinng!

Beck fell into a large brushy thatch of leaves on the end of an outstretched branch. The tangle of bristly leaves scratched. But one twig caught on her tunic so that she didn't fall.

Crash! Boom! Riiip!

The sled came tumbling after her. It fell through the branches, ripping and tearing until it landed in pieces on the ground below.

Beck blinked. She couldn't believe her luck. She struggled to sit up, but she was stuck. She was going to need help to get loose.

Twitter flew over her in circles. "Are you all r-r-r-right? Are you hurt?"

"I'm fine," Beck said. "Are you?"

"Yes . . . b-b-but . . . I'm sorrrrrry!" Twitter wailed. "The sled is broken and . . . it's my fault."

"No, it's not," Beck told him quickly. She tried to keep the disappointment out of her voice. "It wasn't your fault at all."

"You're not mad at me?"

Beck sighed and shook her head. All

that work. And she had come so close. Now she was back at square one.

She swallowed the lump that was rising in her throat and forced herself to laugh. "Aren't we silly? Look at me. I'm stuck. Do you want to do something for me?"

"Yes," Twitter said quickly. "Yes. Yes. What can I do now?"

"Go tell the others I'm stuck in the . . . in the . . ." Beck looked around. Where was she?

Suddenly, she saw a face appear in a knothole of the tree trunk.

"I don't remember inviting *you* over," said a familiar nasty voice.

Vidia!

She had crashed into Vidia's private

tree. "Tell them I'm stuck in the sour-plum tree," Beck told Twitter. "And I need help."

"All right, Beck. I will. I'll be back as fast as I can." Twitter darted away, leaving Beck stuck in the leaves of Vidia's sour-plum tree.

Vidia flew toward Beck. She held out her hand. "Here. I'll get you out." She took Beck's hands and pulled hard.

"*Ouch!*" Beck cried.

The leaves of the sour-plum tree scratched Beck's arms and legs when Vidia pulled her from the tangle. But Vidia didn't seem to care. "Well, don't bother to be grateful or anything, sweetie." Vidia put her hands on her hips. "Lucky for you, darling, I happened to be home and saw your little spill."

"I-I-I'm grateful," Beck stuttered. She always felt shy around Vidia.

Vidia called everybody sweetie and darling. But Vidia felt affection for no one—except herself. And everybody in Pixie Hollow knew it. She didn't like the other fairies and they didn't like her—

which was why she didn't live in the Home Tree with the others. She lived by herself in the sour-plum tree.

Vidia waved Beck's thanks away. "Don't mention it. We'll just say that you owe me a favor. What were you doing in that sled-thing, anyway?"

"Trying to fly with the birds," Beck said, blushing. Even to her own ears, it sounded very silly.

Vidia lifted an eyebrow. "Is that so? Why do you want to fly with the birds?"

"Because I want to explore," Beck blurted out. "I want to see what's outside Pixie Hollow."

A slow smile spread over Vidia's face. Her eyes lit up. She leaned closer. "I don't blame you. If I had to stay in Pixie

Hollow all the time, I'd go crazy. Why *shouldn't* you shake the dirt of this place off your boots? Why *shouldn't* you see the big world?"

"If only I were a fast-flying fairy." Beck sighed. "But even if I were, I wouldn't be able to fly very far away and still come back."

"You could if you were willing to bend a few rules. Some of us do, you know. Wait here." Vidia ran lightly to the knothole in the tree and ducked into the trunk. A few moments later, she came out. She was holding a small velvet sack.

Beck backed up. Everyone knew that Vidia had her own extra-powerful fairy dust. It was made out of feathers that

Vidia had plucked from Mother Dove. Plucking feathers from Mother Dove was forbidden. It was the worst thing a fairy could do. As a result, Vidia had been banished from Mother Dove's home. She was not allowed near the hawthorn tree.

Vidia pressed the small velvet sack into Beck's hand. "Feel the weight. Did you ever dream of so much fairy dust? There's enough dust here to take you to the other side of the world and back. I'll give it to you if you promise to tell no one."

"No!" Beck protested. "I could never—"

Vidia cut her off. "I know. I know. You're Mother Dove's special pet, and you'd never do anything to hurt her. But this dust came from a feather plucked years ago. Why shouldn't you use it? It's not like it would hurt her now."

Beck chewed her lip. There was some truth in what Vidia said. "Why would you help me?" Beck asked.

Vidia draped her arm over Beck's shoulders. "Because I like you. You've got spunk. You want more out of life than hanging around Pixie Hollow. There are plenty of animal-talent fairies around. Plenty of every kind of fairy. Let's face it. Most of them are just taking up tree space. How many fairies does it really take to pop the dings out of pots and fold napkins?"

"But—"

Vidia ignored her. "Fairies like you and me are independent. We want to be more than just another fairy. We want to *fly faster.*"

Beck couldn't help feeling flattered. She'd never really thought of herself as independent.

Vidia winked at her. "Take it and go."

"No. I can't. I . . ." Beck tried to give the sack back to Vidia, but Vidia shot up into the air.

"Catch me if you can," she said with a laugh.

Beck stretched her wings and flew as hard as she could. Vidia might fly faster, but Beck had to catch her and return the sack.

Vidia pointed toward the horizon,

where another flock of Explorer Birds moved through the sky with dizzying speed. She zoomed back and flew circles around Beck. "This is your chance, Beck. Fly away. See the world. Go! Go! *Go!*"

With that, Vidia threw a handful of sparkling dust into the air. The dust twinkled as it rained down on Beck's head and shoulders.

Beck felt a jolt of power surge through her wings. It lifted her through the air and shot her forward toward the flock. It was like a dream. Never had she flown so fast. Never had it been so easy.

She was gaining on them. She could catch up. And once she caught up, she would keep up. *I'm going!* Beck decided in a burst of joy. *I'm going!*

"Good-bye!" she heard Vidia call out behind her.

Beck waved her hand in the direction of Pixie Hollow. "Good-bye!"

5

BECK SLIPPED into the back of the birds' formation. It took her only seconds to match her wing motion with theirs. She felt as if she could fly for hours. For days. For weeks.

She checked the side of her tunic. The little velvet sack was heavy. Full of dust. Enough dust to take her to the other side of the world and back, Vidia had said. Beck felt a sharp stab of guilt. What would Mother Dove think of her if she knew that Beck was using dust made from illegally plucked feathers?

But when Beck looked down, her happiness grew so large that it pushed the guilt to the back of her heart. She was flying higher than she had ever flown.

Down below she saw rivers and mountains. Plains and forests. Never Land was bigger than she had ever dreamed.

"Wait a minute! You're not one of us." The bird flying beside Beck stared. "You're not even a bird."

"I'm a fairy," Beck explained. "My name is Beck."

The bird was so surprised that he

bumped into the bird ahead of him. That bird bumped into the bird ahead of her. And *that* bird bumped into . . . Well, you get the picture. Pretty soon, the whole formation had fallen apart.

The flock leader noticed the problem and led them downward. Beck followed, determined to stay with the flock.

The birds settled in the treetops, chattering and curious. What had happened? What had gone wrong? Why were they stopping?

One by one, the birds began to notice Beck. And when they did, they fell silent. After a few moments, every single bird in the flock was staring at her.

The flock leader flew over and eyed her. His cheeping was curt and clear. "You're a fairy, aren't you?"

Beck nodded. "That's right."

"What are you doing this far from Pixie Hollow?"

"I want to travel. I want to go exploring with you," Beck said.

"What fun!" the bird to Beck's left chirped. "You can be our mascot. We'll be the only flock of Explorer Birds with a fairy. The others will be *so* jealous."

"Wait, not so fast," clucked another. "This sounds like trouble to me. She's already ruined one flight pattern. How do we know she won't do it all the time?"

The birds broke into excited chatter. Some wanted to keep her. But lots of others were worried. "What if she can't learn the flock formations?" "What if she can't find her own food?" "What if she can't keep up?"

Flying so far so fast had given Beck enough confidence to speak up. "I didn't spoil your flight pattern. *He* did." She pointed to the bird who had been beside her. "That's because he was surprised to see me. But it won't happen again. I've been flying with you for a while and you never even noticed. I think I've proven that I can keep up."

The flock leader cocked his head, and his eye gleamed. "You have a point. But you can't blame us for not wanting to take a chance. Today was just ordinary flying. Nothing fancy. But the skies are full of hawks, headwinds, and hail. We have to use some different tricks to survive sometimes. How do we know you can do it?"

"Try me," Beck challenged.

The flock leader nodded. "Very well. Follow me." He shot into the air so fast, all Beck saw was a streak of blue and yellow. Within seconds, he was yards above her.

Beck reached into the sack and sprinkled her wings with the extra-powerful fairy dust.

Varooom! Beck's wings beat the air so hard they made a whipping sound behind her. She trailed the flock leader for a few seconds, checking the wind. Then she lowered her head and poured on the speed. The gap between the flock leader and Beck narrowed until she was flying steadily by his left wing.

The flock leader moved sharply to the right. Beck hadn't seen it coming. She turned to catch up. But he had already changed course again.

Beck gritted her teeth and zoomed. Once again, she centered herself by his left wing. As soon as she did, he rolled and dropped. He left her flying alone.

Beck took some deep breaths. This was going to be harder than she'd thought.

She needed more than the ability to fly fast. She needed her own talent. Animal talents didn't communicate with animals only by speaking their languages.

Beck closed her eyes for a moment. She struggled to force her mind to connect with the flock leader's. She felt a flicker. A flutter. A sudden lightness of heart and quickness of thought. She didn't "hear" him thinking. But she knew what was in his mind.

She banked and barrel-rolled. She dropped until once again she was flying at his left wing.

This time, when he headed straight upward and fell in a tailslide, she matched his movement exactly. When he stopped and slipped backward through the air, the distance between his wing and Beck's didn't vary an inch.

He banked. She banked. He tilted to the right. So did she. He sped up. Beck did, too.

She could feel his approval. He was having fun now, and so was she. Together, they flew faster and faster. They did figure eights and loops, back turns and barrel rolls. Finally, he headed downward with Beck at his left wing. They landed together on a tree limb.

"Welcome to the flock," the leader told her.

6

THE NEXT FEW DAYS were glorious.
Every morning, the Explorer Birds took
to the sky. And when they saw something interesting or exciting or new, they
stopped to check it out.

Beck got to know many of the birds
by name: Ugo, Wego, Uway, Awayme,
Ugone, and Hewent. But her special
friend was Igo.

"Look down there," said Igo. "It's the Striped Sea."

Beck looked and drew in her breath sharply. The waves were striped! She saw a pink-and-white-striped wave followed by a blue-striped wave followed by a yellow-striped wave. "It's true!" Beck exclaimed. "There really *is* a Striped Sea. Some fairies thought it was a tall tale."

"Of course there's a Striped Sea," Igo answered. "Everybody knows that. It's the last big body of water before the Roughtongue Desert."

The flock began to head downward. "Speaking of . . . it looks like we're going to stop there for lunch. Good. You haven't lived until you've tasted Roughtongue plums."

The Explorer Birds landed on a large stretch of desert dotted with lacy trees. Each tree was full of tiny plump plums. Beck picked one and landed lightly on the ground. Might as well take this chance to stretch her legs.

"Hellllooooooo . . ."

Beck jumped at the strange voice—a voice that wasn't really a voice. A voice that was like a rattle and a sigh.

"Wheeeeere are you goooooing? Are you lossssssssst?"

Beck felt the sand below her move. She smiled. It was the sand talking, just as Spinner had said. "Thank you very much," she said politely. "But we're just taking a short lunch break. Then we'll be flying away."

"Flyyyyyyyying? Are you a bird? You don't look like a biiiiiirrrrrrrd."

"No. I'm a fairy," Beck said.

"Issssssss that like a ssssssparrrrrrow man? I met a sssssssparrrow mannnnn oncccccce." The sand shifted and rippled. A soft dune rose in front of Beck. Then, magically, a face shaped out of sand appeared in the side of the dune. It stared at Beck curiously.

"Yes! A sparrow man is a boy pixie. I think I know who you mean. His name is Spinner. Do you know where he is?" Beck asked.

The dune collapsed and rose again behind Beck. She whirled around and saw squiggly lines scrawl across the side of the sand—like a map. A little picture of an oasis with an X on it appeared. "The oassssssiiissssss. Do you want me to ssshowww you how to get thhhhhere?"

The flock leader whistled. It was time to move on. "I wish I had time. But I have to leave," Beck told the sand. "But . . . but . . . if you see Spinner, tell him hello from Pixie Hollow."

A wind blew across the sand, and the map, dune, and face were gone. "I willlllllll," the sand sighed. "I promisssse."

Beck hurried to join the others. The flock rose into the sky and pinwheeled away.

Beck had never felt so happy in her life. The world was an amazing place. And she wanted to see every single inch of it.

For the next hour or so, the flock flew at an easy pace over forests and hilltops. Igo flew on Beck's right. They cheeped and chatted as they flew. But then a sharp clucking from the front of the flock warned Beck to pay close attention. She fixed her eyes on the bird in the lead, and suddenly—*whoosh*—the entire formation shot straight upward.

Whizzzzz!

Beck felt something slice through the air beneath them.

Another series of clucks warned her that the flock was about to turn again. This time, the flock dropped through the air.

Whizzzzz!

Something cold sliced through the air overhead.

"What is that?" Beck asked.

But Igo didn't answer. There were no cheeps or birdcalls of any kind. The air was tense and silent except for the screaming noise of the moving objects that seemed to come out of nowhere.

Every bird was on high alert for signals from their leader.

Suddenly, they flew into air that was dark and freezing cold.

Now Beck understood why the flock leader had tested her skills. The flock zigzagged through the sky. With each move, they just missed being hit by something hurtling through the sky. Finally, Beck realized that they were dodging shards of flying ice. Each shard was huge, sharp, and deadly.

The wind was strong. But the flock flew on and on. It was so dark now that Beck could see only the tail of the bird ahead. It took every bit of flying skill she had to stay with the flock.

Whizzz! Zoooom! Phhhhheewww!

Beck's heart thundered in her chest.

But she wasn't afraid. She had complete faith in the flock leader . . . and in herself. Her ability to stay in formation would keep her—and the birds around her—safe.

Finally, they left the dark and icy cloud. Little by little, the air turned warmer. Beck could feel the flock begin to relax.

Igo let out a series of relieved peeps. "That was a sheet-ice storm. I hate those. They scare me to death."

Beck couldn't help smiling. She wasn't scared. She was ready for the next adventure.

7

BECK! BECK! Where are you?

Beck jerked awake. These days, she slept like a bird, nestled in the notch of a tree with her head tucked beneath her arm.

Beck!

A voice was calling out to her. Was it Igo? No. Her little blue and yellow friend slept peacefully beside her. She saw the tip of his beak peeking out from under his velvety wing.

Beck! Beck! Where are you?

Was it the sand? The breeze? Where was it coming from?

Beck! Beck!

She felt a great trembling in her chest—and suddenly she understood. She wasn't *hearing* the voice. She was *feeling* the voice. And it was coming from inside her very own heart.

It was a voice she knew and loved. It was the voice of Mother Dove.

Beck blinked her eyes. The sun was coming up in the distance. The Explorer Birds began to wake up and start their morning activities. Some of the birds bathed in the morning dew. Some of them breakfasted on berries and acorns. They laughed and joked. All of them were carefree and happy.

The voice in Beck's heart was growing stronger, more insistent. Mother Dove was trying to tell her something. Beck closed her eyes, ready now to listen.

"Ohhhhhh!" she moaned. A wave of pain sent her reeling off the branch. She opened her wings and made a safe landing. But the pain had given her such a shock, she could hardly stand.

Igo came fluttering to join her. "Beck! What's the matter? What is it?"

Beck took some deep breaths. She tried to calm herself. "Something is wrong. Something is wrong with Mother Dove. I have to go home, Igo."

"Why?" her new friend squawked. "I thought you were happy with us."

"I have been," Beck answered. "But Mother Dove needs me. She's in pain. And she's afraid. I have to go. I have to go right away. Tell the others for me, will you?"

"Don't you want to say good-bye?" Igo asked.

Beck shook her head. "No. I'm tired of good-byes. Just tell them . . . tell them . . . thank you for a wonderful adventure."

She leaned forward and kissed Igo on the tip of his beak.

Then she plunged into the air, heading back toward Pixie Hollow.

Beck flew all day and all night.

Whenever her wings faltered, she sprinkled herself with dust. She was exhausted, but she had to get home.

Being alone gave her a chance to think about the messages she had received. She knew now what had caused Mother Dove's moment of fear and pain. Someone had plucked one of her magic feathers.

Vidia!

How could I have been so foolish? she wondered. *Why didn't I see the truth? No wonder Vidia was so eager to help me leave! She knew I took special care of Mother Dove. With me out of the way, she had a perfect shot to pluck a feather.*

Beck felt another kind of pain— shame. Vidia's extra-powerful fairy dust was made from feathers stolen from Mother Dove. How could Beck *ever* have agreed to use Vidia's dust? Now the damage was done, though. Beck *had* to use it—like it or not.

She reached for the sack on her hip. It still felt heavy and full. That was good. She was going to need every speck.

Beck looked down. She was crossing an ocean. It wasn't the Striped Sea, with its friendly-looking, colorful waves. It was the dark, dangerous ocean that divided Never Land from the rest of the world.

The sight made her dizzy. She realized that her dust was wearing out. She reached into the sack for another handful of dust, and her fingertips felt something odd. Down in the bottom of the sack, something was mixed with the dust.

Gravel!

Beck gasped. No wonder the sack was so heavy. It wasn't full of dust. It had been weighted with tiny pieces of rock to make it seem fuller than it was.

Vidia had said, *There's enough dust*

here to take you to the other side of the world and back!

Enough to take her to the other side of the world? Yes. But not nearly enough to get back.

Beck's shock gave way to despair. Vidia had tricked her even more cleverly than Beck had realized. She didn't want Beck gone for a while. She wanted her gone for good.

Well, it wasn't going to work. Beck reached into the sack to find out exactly how much dust was left. If there was just enough to get her to the end of the ocean, she would run—not walk—every step of the way back. But Beck's hands were trembling. And when she tried to reach into the sack, *she dropped it!*

"*No!*" she yelled.

The sack fell down, down, down, into the dark water.

Beck's heart lurched with fear. How would she get back now? Her head spun. Her shoulders ached, and her arms were limp with fatigue. She had been flying for hours, and still the ocean stretched out beneath her. *I can't keep going,* she thought. *I can't.*

She barely managed to stay above the waves. She was so close to the water, she could feel the ocean spray on her wings. They were soaking up moisture and growing heavy. It was becoming impossible to fly.

Lower and lower she dropped. Just as the weight of her wings was about

to drag her under the water, she heard something shriek. A seagull! He was bearing down on her with his beak open.

"I'm not a fish!" Beck shouted. She tried to be heard over the crashing waves. "I'm not a fish! I'm not a— *yeooowww!*"

The seagull's beak snapped at her. It jerked her up just before the water closed over her.

8

THE SEAGULL CARRIED BECK high into the air. She twisted frantically in the grip of his beak.

"Stop wriggling! I'm not trying to eat you," the seagull cawed (though he was hard to understand since his mouth was full—of Beck). "I've been on the lookout for you all night. All the gulls have."

Beck went limp. She was too stunned to struggle anymore. "You have?"

"Yes! We were told you would be traveling this way. Heard you might have some trouble crossing the ocean."

"How? Who told you?"

"Well, the Explorer Birds told the forest birds. And the forest birds told the mountain birds. The mountain birds told the desert birds. And the desert birds told us. Say, you're awfully wet. Let me see if I can get some of that water out of your wings." The seagull shook Beck like a rag. "There! Better?"

"Much better," Beck agreed after her ears stopped ringing. Even though she was out of dust—and didn't much enjoy being shaken like a rag—she couldn't help feeling safer with dry wings.

"Land ho!" cackled the gull. He began gliding downward.

A few moments later, he dropped Beck on the shore of Never Land. She hit the ground with a thump.

She didn't complain, though. She was too grateful to be safely across the water.

A gray rabbit hopped out from behind some brush. "I thought you'd never get here," he said. "I've been worried sick. Are you Beck?"

Beck nodded.

The rabbit hunched down. "Climb up. We're late."

The gull gave Beck a nod. "Go on. Hurry."

Beck climbed onto the back of the gray rabbit.

"You can hang on to my ears. I don't mind," said the rabbit.

"Oh, no!" Beck said. "I couldn't."

"Have you ever ridden a rabbit before?" he asked.

"No."

"Didn't think so," he said. And with that, he bounded forward.

Beck rocked dangerously back and forth, then grabbed for his ears. "Well," she said, hanging on for dear life, "if you *really* don't mind . . ."

After what felt like hours of leaping, the rabbit screeched to a halt. The stop was

so sudden, Beck lost her grip on his ears.
She tumbled forward over his head.

"I'm so sorry." The rabbit leaned
down. His wiggling pink nose checked
her for damage. "I should have warned

you that I was going to stop. But I get forgetful when I'm nervous."

"Nervous about what?" Beck asked.

"No need to be nervous," said a silken voice.

The rabbit's quivering nose froze. "That's what," he whispered.

A large fox stepped toward them. Beck froze, too. Foxes could be dangerous. Especially if they were hungry.

The fox sat back on her haunches and gave them both a smile. "You can trust me. I've sworn on Mother Dove's egg that I will not harm either one of you. I'm going to take you on the last part of your journey," she said to Beck.

"They told me to tell you that you can trust her," the rabbit whispered.

"Who?" Beck whispered back.

"Can't remember. I told you I get forgetful when I'm nervous. Well, good luck!" And with that, the rabbit scampered away as fast as his legs could carry him.

Now, riding a fox is not at all like riding a rabbit. At first, Beck was so frightened, she didn't even notice the fox's smooth gait. She gingerly held on to the fox's ruff. She wouldn't have touched her ears for a million pounds of fairy dust.

"No need to be scared," the fox said as they slid through the forest. "I would never hurt an animal-talent fairy."

"Why not?" Beck asked. She was

too nervous to try to read the fox's thoughts.

"An animal-talent fairy saved my cubs once during a flood," the fox answered. "I sent word to Mother Dove that if an animal-talent fairy ever needed me, I would be there to help."

"Mother Dove knows I'm coming?" Beck gasped.

"Of course," the fox answered.

Just ahead, a glimmer of sunlight appeared between the trees of the dark forest. It was Pixie Hollow! Two fairies hovered at the edge. They nervously peered into the dark forest.

"Tink! Terence!" Beck jumped off the fox's back and ran as fast as she could the rest of the way. Her friends landed on the ground and opened their arms. Beck threw herself into their joyful embrace.

"HELLO!" they shouted. "WELCOME HOME!"

9

BECK HAD GROWN CLEVER during her travels. Her first question was "Who else knows I'm here?"

"No one except Mother Dove and the animal-talent fairies," Tink answered.

"Let's keep it that way for now," Beck said. "How is Mother Dove?"

Tink shook her head. "Fine, so far.

But someone has plucked two feathers from her."

"*Two* feathers!" Beck wailed. "But how?"

"Nobody knows. The first time it happened, Queen Clarion posted scouts in every tree around the hawthorn. No one could fly near the nest without being spotted. But somehow . . . they did."

Beck pressed her lips together tightly. "I don't know how she's doing it, but I do know *who* is doing it. And I'm going to catch her red-handed."

Beck's reunion with Mother Dove was secret.

No one in Pixie Hollow ever knew

what they said to each other. But for years afterward, everyone talked about how Mother Dove's happiness created a sense of peace in Pixie Hollow that made the fairies extra kind for days.

But that first night, when Beck hid in Mother Dove's nest and snuggled next to her, Beck was angry and afraid. She thought she knew who was stealing Mother Dove's feathers. But what if she was wrong? What if they never caught the feather thief? Mother Dove slept happily, knowing that Beck was back at her side. But Beck had one eye open, waiting.

She didn't have to wait long. She heard an almost silent sound. Someone was coming toward the nest. And she wasn't flying—she was climbing.

Beck watched as a hand reached up and grabbed the side of the nest. Vidia pulled herself over the edge. She leaned forward to pluck one of Mother Dove's feathers.

Beck made her move. She flew at Vidia so fiercely that Vidia let out a startled scream and fell backward out of the nest. She fluttered her wings and caught her balance. But before she could escape, Beck had called the scouts.

They came from every side and surrounded Vidia.

"I was right. It was you," Beck said, pointing at the fast-flying fairy.

"But how?" the others asked. "How did she get so close?"

Beck flew down and landed on

the ground. She walked around the hawthorn, looking for something. She leaned over and lifted a small stone. Under it was a dark hole. "The animal-talent tunnels," Beck said. "Vidia must have found out how to get to the tree from underground. She knew you would be expecting her to fly. So she came below the ground, climbed the tree, and stole two feathers."

Vidia shrugged. "So you caught me trying to take one tonight. But *I* didn't steal the other two feathers."

"Then who did?" asked a scout.

"Beck!" declared Vidia.

"What!" Beck cried.

"*You* did, and now you're trying to blame it on me."

Beck couldn't think of anything to say. "Why would I steal feathers?" she managed to squeak.

"Because you wanted more than your fair share of dust. You wanted to be a fast-flying-talent fairy. You wanted to travel. You knew you could steal the feathers and I would be blamed. Because I get blamed for everything. But not this time, sweetie."

More fairies had shown up. Beck noticed they were all looking at her strangely.

"She *did* want to fly faster," a sparrow man said.

"And she sure tried everything else," a cooking-talent fairy pointed out. "Remember the wing extenders?"

"Remember the sleigh?" Twire said with a gasp.

Suddenly, everyone was talking at once. To her horror, Beck realized that she *did* look guilty. This was terrible. Beck had risked everything to come back and catch the feather thief. Only now everybody thought the feather thief was Beck.

She took a deep breath and shook her head. She wasn't shy-and-frightened little Beck anymore. She had seen the world. She had flown across the Striped Sea and talked to the Roughtongue sand. She had dangled from the beak of a seagull, bucked along on the back of a rabbit, and traveled through the darkest part of the forest with a she-fox.

So why was she letting Vidia push her around?

Enough already. "QUIET!" Beck ordered.

Every fairy fell silent.

Beck pointed at Vidia. "I know that you stole the feathers. You gave me a velvet sack full of dust. You said it was enough dust to fly to the other side of the world and back. But you lied. You weighted the sack with gravel. You hoped I'd never come back so you would be free to keep stealing feathers."

Vidia smirked. "Easy to say. Hard to prove."

"I know how you can prove you're innocent," Terence said to Beck. "Show us the sack."

"Yes. Yes. Show us the sack," the other fairies echoed.

Beck's heart sank. The sack was probably at the bottom of the ocean. She felt a lump rising in her throat. If she said she dropped it in the ocean, no one would believe her.

A sudden noise overhead drew everyone's attention to the sky. Winged creatures of all sizes and shapes were coming to Pixie Hollow from every direction.

10

FLOCKS OF BIRDS landed in the trees and bushes. Explorer Birds, gulls, pelicans, and sparrows. Toucans, parakeets, falcons, woodpeckers, and mockingbirds.

The noise was deafening. Once they all had landed, a signal from an ancient parrot kept them quiet. A pelican opened his bill. The parrot reached in and removed a small wet velvet sack.

Beck gasped. "That's the sack Vidia gave me. How did you find it?"

The parrot dropped the sack and gave an animated series of squawks.

Fawn stepped forward and offered to translate for the non-animal-talent fairies. "He says the sack was caught by a passing seagull. The gull gave it to the pelican, who'd heard about the fairy who dropped it from another seagull, who had talked to a forest bird, who had talked to a desert bird, who had talked to a mountain bird. When we figured out that this belonged to the fairy who flew across Never Land with the Explorer Birds, we knew we had to bring it back."

Vidia lifted her chin. "You can't prove that belongs to me."

Terence lifted the sack and studied it. "I think we can. It seems to have your name on it." The fairies surged around Terence to look at the sack.

Suddenly, several fairies stepped back. Queen Clarion had arrived.

Queen Clarion took the sack from Terence and fingered the stitched name. "This sack does belong to Vidia. I know because I gave it to her a long time ago, back when she was still a friend. I had hoped she would stay a friend."

Vidia rolled her eyes.

"Beck is telling the truth," Queen Clarion said. "The feather thief is Vidia!" She stretched out her hand and pointed an accusing finger at Vidia. "Vidia, for once you're going to pay the price for your deeds. Consider yourself grounded—literally. No flying for two weeks."

Vidia sneered. "Try to stop me." She took off, climbing into the air. But she didn't get far. Two sparrows streaked up, cutting her off. Vidia changed direction. But a flock of parakeets working together forced her down.

Vidia was going to have to take her medicine. Birds of every feather were making sure that Vidia, the fast-flying fairy, would spend the next two weeks on the ground.

"So there really is a Striped Sea? And you really did talk to the sand?" Terence asked.

Beck nodded. "Yes. I saw all those things with my own eyes. Terence, there are amazing things in the world. I don't know why you ever doubted it."

Terence and Beck were sitting beside Havendish Stream. Terence shook his head. "Golly. I didn't believe poor Spinner. But I do now."

"Did somebody call me?" A sparrow man came walking along the bank of the stream. He had reddish blond hair that stuck out in every direction. His tunic was frayed and faded, and there were holes in his boots. He looked as if he had been walking for a long time. But he didn't seem the least bit unhappy. His grin was wide and friendly.

"Spinner!" Terence gasped. "It's

you. Where have you been all these years?" He jumped up and gave his friend a hug.

Spinner grinned. "I heard that somebody from Pixie Hollow said to tell me hello, and I realized I was homesick. So I decided to come back for a visit."

"But how did you get here?" Beck gasped.

Spinner hitched his thumbs into the armholes of his tunic and took a deep breath. "Well, it's sort of a long story. A friend of mine told me where the pirates went to pick coconuts. So I went there and found a coconut with a hole in it. I hid myself in that coconut and waited. Sure enough, along came some pirates to gather coconuts. Those pirates loaded

me onto their pirate ship. They never had any idea at all that I was aboard. As soon as we hit the shore, I—"

Terence cut him off with a loud laugh. "Oh, Spinner. You never change. That sounds like another one of your tall tales. What do you think, Beck?"

Beck smiled. "Maybe it is. Maybe it isn't. All I know is that the only thing as good as *having* an adventure is *hearing* about one." Beck patted a toadstool, inviting Spinner to sit beside her. "So tell us, Spinner," she said, handing him a cookie, "what happened next?"

The Trouble with Tink

Just then, they heard a metallic creaking sound. Suddenly—*plink, plink, plink, plink!* One by one, tiny streams of water burst through the damaged copper. The pot looked more like a watering can than something to boil dye in.

"Oh!" Violet and Terence gasped. They turned to Tink, their eyes wide.

Tink felt herself blush, but she couldn't tear her eyes away from the leaking pot. She had never failed to fix a pot before, much less made it worse than it was when she got it.

The thing was, no fairy ever failed at her talent. To do so would mean you weren't really talented at all.

Don't miss any of the magical
Disney Fairies chapter books!

Vidia and the Fairy Crown

All eyes turned toward Vidia, who crossed her arms and shifted her weight from one foot to the other. She scowled across the fairy circle at Rani and Tink.

"Well?" said Queen Ree, turning to look at Vidia. "Is that true? Did you say that, Vidia?"

"I said that I wasn't coming to the party," Vidia replied. "I think my exact words were 'unless, of course, you need someone to fly in and snatch that gaudy crown off high-and-mighty Queen Ree's head.'"

The crowd gasped. To say such a thing—and right in front of the queen herself!

Prilla and the Butterfly Lie

An uncomfortable silence filled the tearoom. Some fairies studied their forks. Others examined their dinner plates very closely. No one would look up.

"No volunteers," said the queen. "This is indeed a problem. What are we to do?"

"I know!" said a voice. "There is a fairy who would be happy to help out. She *loves* butterflies."

The room began to buzz once more. Everyone wondered who the butterfly-loving fairy could be.

Prilla sank into her chair until her head was barely level with the table. She had completely forgotten about her butterfly lie.

Tink, North of Never Land

Inside, she slammed the door behind her. When that didn't make her feel better, she kicked over the basket of rivets. They rolled to every corner of her tidy workshop, which only made Tink's temper worse.

"Every time I see Terence, he ignores me!" she fumed. She paced in the air. "Why, he practically goes out of his way to avoid me. And he hasn't been by to visit since . . . since . . ."

Oh.

Tink sat down with a thump. Finally, it dawned on her: she'd told Terence to leave her alone, and that was exactly what he was doing.

DISNEY FAIRIES

Believing is just the beginning...

Discover the magical world of Disney Fairies.

The Trouble with Tink

Beck and the Great Berry Battle

Vidia and the Fairy Crown

Lily's Pesky Plant

Fira and the Full Moon

Rani in the Mermaid Lagoon

A Masterpiece for Bess

Prilla and the Butterfly Lie

Tink, North of Never Land

Beck Beyond the Sea

COLLECT THEM ALL!

Available wherever books are sold.
Also available on audio.

  RANDOM HOUSE CHILDREN'S BOOKS